3800 17 0014463 1

HIGH LIFE HIGHLAND

D0280723

The Dragon's Bride

Dragons

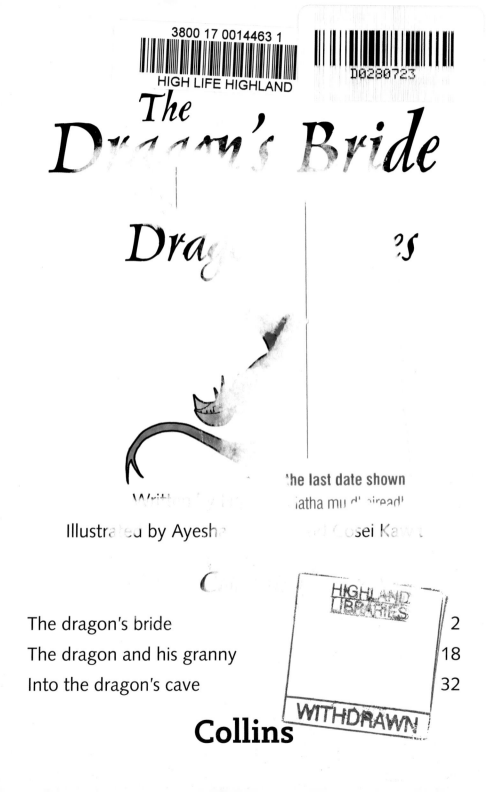

the last date shown
iatha mu d' iread

Illustrated by Ayesha

osei Ka

HIGHLAND
LIBRARIES

WITHDRAWN

Collins

The dragon's bride

A story from Scandinavia

Oh no! The queen was crying, again. What was the matter?
She was wise. She was kind. She was rich. She was beautiful.
She lived in a fine castle. She loved her husband, the king.
Her life seemed perfect. But she didn't have a baby, and that
was what she longed for. And so every day, day after day,
the queen cried.

"My dear," said the king, "how I wish I could help you! Please try to stop crying, just for a while. Why not go for a walk in the forest? The fresh air might make you feel better."

The queen sat under a tree and listened to the birds singing. They sounded happy. With a long sigh, she whispered to herself, "If only – "

"If only what?"

The sudden noise startled her. She turned and saw an old woman. "If only I had a baby," said the queen. "But no one can help me."

"Hmmm!" mumbled the old woman. "Come closer, and listen."

The old woman whispered, "Go to the castle gardens.
There, you'll see two magic roses. Choose one, only
one – and eat it!"

Late that night, back at the castle, the queen found the roses.
They glowed gently in the dark, and smelt wonderful.
Which should she choose? She couldn't decide. So she
ate two!

A few months later, the queen discovered that she was going to have a baby. She was delighted! So was the king – but he had to go away.

"Take care, my dear," he said, kissing the queen goodbye. "I'll be back soon to welcome our new little prince or princess."

Poor king! Poor queen! Their hopes and dreams soon turned into a nightmare. Because, when the baby was born, it wasn't a prince. And it wasn't a princess. It was a DRAGON. The dragon grew and grew, becoming more snake-like and savage. Soon, it was bigger than the queen and stronger than the soldiers guarding the castle.

When the king came home, the dragon snapped its terrifying teeth, and demanded: "You must love me as your son, or I'll bite off your head and knock down your castle."

Year by year, the dragon grew even bigger and more dangerous. One day, he said to the king, "I'm grown up now. I want to get married. Find me a bride!"

In fear of his life, the king wrote to other royal families. Would anyone marry his son, he asked – without meeting him? Amazingly, two princesses agreed.

The dragon married the first bride and they had
a splendid wedding. The king welcomed his guests to
a wonderful feast with music and singing and dancing.

But then, once the guests had gone, the dragon gobbled
up the princess – quick as a flash!

At the second wedding, everyone was very nervous.
Soldiers guarded the bride. But – guess what? The dragon
ate her, too!

A few days later, the dragon said again, "Find me a bride!"

The king didn't know what to do. Now everyone knew that his son was a dragon. Who'd marry *that*?

In despair, the king wandered out into the forest. There, he met a shepherd and his daughter, called Maren. The king had a brainwave. Maren could be the dragon's bride!

The shepherd begged, but the king wouldn't change his mind.

Bravely, Maren said, "Don't worry. I'll be fine." Then she went to cry in secret among the forest trees.

"Why so sad?" It was an old woman, suddenly standing beside her.

"No one can help me," sobbed Maren.

"Hmmm," mumbled the old woman. "Come closer, and listen."

Hardly daring to hope, Maren sat down beside her.

Soon, it was the day of the wedding. Maren got up early. As the old woman had told her, she put on ten different dresses, one on top of the other. Then she gave her father a big, brave hug. "Time to go to the castle," she said, trying not to sound nervous.

It was a sad and sorry wedding. Everyone was weeping, except the dragon and Maren. Her heart beat wildly in her chest. But she kept her feelings secret.

The wedding guests left. Night fell. It seemed dreadfully dark, even inside the castle.

"Time for bed," said the dragon, smiling at Maren. The smile showed all his teeth. She'd never seen so many.

In spite of those terrifying teeth, Maren stayed calm.
She remembered what the old woman had said, and spoke
up boldly.

"I'll get ready for bed," she said, smoothing the skirts of her
ten wedding dresses, "if you'll take off your skin."

The dragon was so surprised that he forgot to be bloodthirsty.

"Go on!" said Maren, very quickly, before the dragon
could remember. "Just pull! It's quite easy!"

The dragon pinched and tugged – and a slimy, spiky, scaly layer of skin came away in his teeth! Nine more times, the dragon said, "It's bedtime!" And nine more times, Maren gave him the very same answer.

Nine times, Maren brushed her hair and took off a dress. And, nine times, the dragon peeled away another layer of skin.

Each time, he got smaller and weaker, until …

With a flash and a crash and a bang, the dragon disappeared! Maren found a handsome young prince standing beside her.

The prince explained: "The dragon was my twin brother. We were trapped inside one set of skins when the queen ate both magic roses. But now he's gone, and you've set me free!"

Maren gazed at the prince in wonder. He was as different from the dragon as it was possible to be, and she could see kindness in his eyes.

There was another crash as the king's soldiers broke down the door. But instead of a dragon, they found two very happy people.

"At last, my dear," said the king to the queen, "I think you can stop crying."

The dragon and his granny

A story from Germany

Far away and long ago, there were three best friends.
Their names were Jake, Will and Conrad. Jake was sensible.
Will was a worrier. Conrad was daring. Times were tough in
their home town and so they decided to run away together.

"We'll need to find jobs," said Jake.

"And food … and shelter," said Will.

"Boring!" said Conrad. "I want to find fame and fortune and have adventures."

At first, all went well. But, by wintertime, the friends were in trouble. They were cold and wet – and homeless and hungry and frightened.

"Do you think we'll die?" groaned Will, as they sheltered under some bushes.

"Well, not right now," said Jake. "But … WHAT'S THAT? HIDE! GET DOWN!"

Red, roaring flames lit up the world. There was hissing and sizzling and a terrible smell of burning.

Conrad was the first to look around.
He could hardly believe
his eyes. It was a real
live dragon!

"Good afternoon!"
the dragon said.
"Why are you hiding?"

"Why do you think?" said Conrad. "We're scared!"

"We've never met a dragon before," explained Jake, rather more politely.

"It's your roaring I don't like," whispered Will.

"Why aren't you at home?" the dragon said, kindly. "Or at work, or at school?"

The friends told him.

"But I can help you!" the dragon replied. "Here's a magic wand. It makes gold. Try it!"

Amazed and excited, Conrad waved the wand, and sure enough, a pile of gold coins appeared at his feet.

"But beware!" said the dragon. "That wand comes with a terrible price."

"Take it back, then!" cried Will.

"Too late!" snarled the dragon. "Enjoy the gold! But in seven years' time, you must pay the price for my help. I'll make you my slaves – for ever!" Then he flapped his wicked wings and flew off into the sky.

The friends stamped and raged, but the dragon didn't hear them.

"Let's use the wand, anyway!" said Conrad. "With gold, life will be good – for a while." So the boys had many exciting adventures, but all too soon, the seven years ended.

"We're doomed!" wailed Will. "I'm so frightened!"

Out of nowhere, an old woman appeared, and asked what the matter was. "Foolish boys, wicked dragon!" she said, when they explained. "Now, this is what you must do. One of you must go to the deep, dark heart of the forest. You must find a rock that looks like a house – and squeeze through its hidden door, into the unknown! There, you'll find the help you need."

"Sounds risky," said Jake.

"I'd be terrified," said Will.

"I'll go!" said Conrad.
"It'll be an adventure!"

The forest was full of stabbing thorns, tangling roots and threatening noises. But at last, Conrad reached the rock. He went towards it, opened the door, stepped inside – and suddenly found himself falling, falling …

Dizzy and breathless, Conrad looked around. He was in a strange underground house – and someone was waiting for him! It was the old woman.

"Welcome!" she said. "I'm the dragon's granny."

Conrad watched, astonished, as the frail old granny heaved up a huge stone from the floor. Beneath it, steps led down into the darkness.

"Under there! Keep quiet! And listen!" she said, and pushed the stone down on top of him.

"ROAAAR!" The dragon arrived for tea. He munched and crunched and, with a mean, nasty laugh, told his granny how he planned to take the friends to his fearsome, fiery kingdom.

"I'll give them one chance to escape," he said. "I'll ask them this riddle:

> I'm a little man in a red, red coat,
>
> With a stick in my hand and a stone in my throat.
>
> Who am I?

They'll never guess the answer. So they'll be my slaves for ever!"

"Let me think," said Granny. "I've got it!" And she shouted out the answer, so loudly that Conrad could hear her.

"Shhhh!" said the dragon, crossly.

Once the dragon had fallen asleep, Granny lifted the stone, helped Conrad climb up, and showed him the quickest way out of the forest.

When Conrad got back from the forest, he found Jake and Will looking terrified.

"Don't worry!" he said. "The dragon won't get us. Trust me!"

"I hope you're right," said Jake. "If not …"

"ROAAAR!" The dragon arrived, grinning horribly.

"Time to be my slaves," he said. "But I'll give you a chance. Guess this riddle, and you can go free:

I'm a little man in a red, red coat,

With a stick in my hand and a stone in my throat.

Who am I?"

Jake made a desperate guess. "Father Christmas?" he said, in a shaky voice.

"I don't know," sighed Will. And he burst into tears.

"Wrong! Wrong! Last chance now!" sneered the dragon.

"A cherry!" shouted Conrad.

The dragon's jaw dropped. "How did you – ?" he started to say, but it was no use; Conrad had given the right answer. Snorting and muttering, he stomped angrily away into the forest.

The friends watched the dragon disappear into the distance. Amazed and delighted, they danced for joy and hugged each other. They were free! They were free!

Into the dragon's cave

A story from Japan

There once was a Japanese warlord who never would
stop fighting. He was brave as a lion, fierce as a dragon and
always angry. So the emperor sent him to live – in peace –
on a faraway island.

The warlord had a daughter called Tokoyo. She was sad
and lonely after her father went away. She said to herself:
"One day I'll find him and bring him home!"

Tokoyo waited and waited, until she could bear the loneliness no longer. She set off to rescue her father, walking for days until she reached the ocean. But the sailors refused to take her to the island. They said that terrible weather – a deadly dragon storm – was coming!

The winds and waves were wild, but nothing would
stop Tokoyo. Late that night, she crept down to the harbour.
She found a boat, and set off for the island.

She rowed all night and all the next day. The dragon storm was frightful. But, at last, she staggered ashore and fell asleep, exhausted. Tomorrow, she hoped, she'd find her father.

Strange noises woke her. Still sleepy, Tokoyo rubbed her eyes. Coming towards her, she saw a wailing girl and an old man. Were they ghosts? Was she dreaming?

"Please, don't be frightened," the old man said, as Tokoyo leapt to her feet in horror. "I can explain.

"A dreadful dragon, Yofune Nushi, lives in the seas around our island. When he gets angry, he whips up storms to wreck our boats and drown our sailors. To keep him happy, we send a girl to visit him every year. Tomorrow, we'll throw her into the sea, to join him."

"Don't do that!" cried Tokoyo. She put her arms around the weeping girl. "Let her stay on the island! I'm a good swimmer, so I'll go in her place to meet the dragon!"

Before anyone could stop her, she dived, deep, deep down.

Tokoyo swam down until she saw the entrance to a splendid cave, glittering with crystals and gleaming with pearls. Then, from deep inside, something snaky and slimy began to slither towards her. It stretched its mighty legs, flexed its cruel claws and blinked its fiery eyes. It was the dragon, Yofune Nushi!

Brave as she was, Tokoyo shivered.

The dragon hadn't yet seen her. Was there time to escape?

But then his mouth opened in a mighty roar, his sharp fangs
flashed, and his jaws crashed and rumbled like thunder.
He reared his giant head and coiled his body like a spring,
ready to attack her!

39

hurling himself towards Tokoyo. "You horrible human! Prepare to die!"

Tokoyo's warlord father had taught her how to fight. Now she needed all her strength and skill, as she struggled to save herself from Yofune Nushi. She punched and kicked and wrestled and strangled. By the end of the battle, Tokoyo was exhausted – but the dragon was dead.

41

Up and up she swam, dragging the dead dragon behind her.
Gasping and shaking, but triumphant, she splashed up to
the surface, where the old man and the girl were still looking
sorrowfully out to sea.

"We thought we'd never see you again!" the old man cried.
"We feared the dragon would kill you! But now you're back.
And what's this here – can it possibly be Yofune Nushi?"

"Don't worry," said Tokoyo. "He can't hurt you now.
Your seas are safe from him. No more dragon storms
or shipwrecks. And," she added, very firmly, "no more girls
pushed into the sea."

Next day, the islanders gave a party to honour Tokoyo, their hero and their friend. Inside his prison cell, Tokoyo's father listened to the happy music and laughter, and smiled.

Far away in his palace, the emperor heard how Tokoyo had saved the islanders from Yofune Nushi. "A girl who kills dragons is something special," he said. "Who is she?"

When his servants told him, the emperor laughed.
"What? Her father's that angry warlord? Well, maybe
she can stop him fighting. Let them be together!
Set him free!"

So Tokoyo and her father went back to their home,
where they lived very happily for a long, long time –
without too many battles.

Wedding bells for "dragon" prince!

The dragon who's been causing so much trouble at the castle has finally gone. Maren, a local shepherd girl, tricked him into removing his scaly skin to free the prince who was trapped inside. Now, she and the prince are married, and the king has declared a day of celebration.

Yofune Nushi is finally killed

For hundreds of years, the islanders have lived in fear of Yofune Nushi. But now he's dead, and they've a new local hero. Yesterday, crowds cheered as dragon-killer Tokoyo and her proud father waved goodbye to the island, and set off together on their long journey home. Who knows what fresh adventures lie ahead for the brave pair?

Dragon tricked by local boys ... with a little help

Today, three friends had a lucky escape from a cruel and cunning dragon, but only because the dragon's very own granny gave them a helping hand. By making sure the boys had the answer to the dragon's very tricky riddle, she set them free.

"We're overjoyed," said the friends. "And now we're rich, as well as happy. We still have the dragon's magic wand, which makes gold, and we plan to have a lot of fun!"

🐾 Ideas for reading 🐾

Written by Clare Dowdall, PhD
Lecturer and Primary Literacy Consultant

Reading objectives:
- increase familiarity with a wide range of books including fairy stories and retell orally
- discuss words and phrases that capture the reader's interest and imagination
- make predictions from details stated and applied

Spoken language objectives:
- participate in discussions, presentations, performances, role play, improvisations and debates

Curriculum links: PSHE – health and wellbeing

Resources: ICT for research; art materials

Build a context for reading

- Ask children to recall facts about dragons from stories that they've read or seen on the screen.
- Look at the front cover. Challenge children to create a list of similes to describe the dragon, e.g. *as scaly as a ...*
- Read the blurb together. Ask children to predict how Maren solves the problem.

Understand and apply reading strategies

- Read pp2–5 to the children. Model how to recount the key information and check that children have understood the problem: that the queen longs for a child.
- Ask children to predict what will happen to the queen who has disobeyed the old woman and eaten two roses, instead of one.
- Ask children to read pp6–7, to see if their predictions are accurate. Then continue reading to find out what happens in this and the other dragon stories.